JJ   **4 WEEKS**   14
Maestro, Giulio
The tortoise's tug of war.

Please Don't Lose the Date Card

The Tortoise's Tug of War

Retold and Illustrated by
GIULIO MAESTRO

BRADBURY PRESS • SCARSDALE, N.Y.

JJ

The story is based on a South American folktale called
WHICH WAS STRONGER, THE TORTOISE, THE TAPIR,
OR THE WHALE?, from a version by C.F. Hartt.

The text of this book is set in 18pt. Garamond Bold.
The illustrations are ink wash and pencil paintings reproduced in full color.

The Tortoise's
Tug of War

One day a Tortoise went walking by the sea
and there he saw a Whale.
"Hey, Whale, play a game with me."

"Nah, you're too small," laughed the Whale.

"Oh, come on," begged the Tortoise.
"I'll play any game you want."

"You're too small for my games," said the Whale,
and he began swimming away from the shore.

"No I'm not," said the Tortoise with a smile.
"I know I can beat you at a tug of war."

"Oh, no you can't," laughed the Whale.

The Tortoise snickered. "Yes I can."

"Then go ahead and try," replied the Whale.

"Okay," said the Tortoise. "Wait here
until I go into the forest and get a sipó."

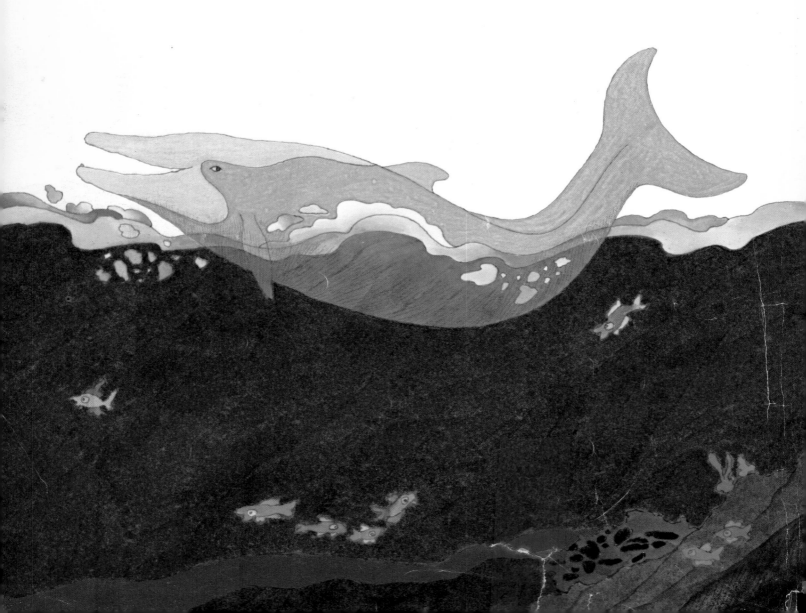

The Tortoise set off toward the forest
and there he met a Tapir.
"Where are you going?" asked the Tapir.

"Into the forest to get a sipó,"
replied the Tortoise.

"And what are you going to do with a sipó?"
asked the Tapir.

"Why, you and I are going to play tug of war
  and I'm going to pull you down to the sea,"
  said the Tortoise.

"You!" laughed the Tapir.
"That's what you think.
  I'll pull you into the forest.
  Get your sipó!"

The Tortoise went off
and came back with a very long sipó.
He tied one end of it around the Tapir.
"Now, for the tug of war," said the Tortoise.
"Wait here while I go down to the sea.
When I shake the sipó, try with all your might
to pull me into the forest."

He then dragged the other end
of the sipó down to the sea and tied it
to the tail of the Whale.
"Now," said the Tortoise, "for the tug of war.
Wait here while I go into the forest.
When I shake the sipó, try with all your might
to pull me into the sea."

Laughing to himself, the Tortoise hid in the bushes
halfway between the Whale and the Tapir
and shook the sipó.

The Whale tugged and tugged.
The Tapir tugged against him.
"That Tortoise is strong," snorted the Whale.

The Tapir tugged and tugged.
The Whale tugged against him.

"I can't budge that Tortoise," groaned the Tapir.
The Whale gained an inch.
But the Tapir tugged back.

After much pulling and tugging
and pulling and tugging
the Whale and the Tapir
could pull and tug no more.

The Tortoise appeared from behind the bushes
and walked down to the sea.
"Well, Tortoise," sighed the Whale,
"I guess you won the tug of war. I'm exhausted."

The Tortoise smiled as he untied the sipó
and walked into the forest
where the Tapir was leaning against a tree.

"Well, Tortoise," gasped the Tapir,
"I guess you won the tug of war. I'm exhausted."

The Tortoise smiled to himself
and dragging the sipó,
he strolled down to the beach.

There he met a Giant Anteater.
"Hey, Anteater, play a game with me."

"Nah, you're too small," the Anteater laughed.

"But I know I can beat you at a tug of war,"
said the Tortoise.

"No you can't," said the Anteater.

"Yes I can," said the Tortoise. "Wait here."

And he went off into the forest
to find a Jaguar to tie to the sipó.